ISBN 979-8-218-22274-1

90000>

9 798218 222741

This book is dedicated to children near and far, who may struggle with sleeping or have bad dreams. Good Boy Lukey represents the ultimate protector of the night and sprinkles his dream crumbs quietly while you sleep – to take all the bad dreams away!! The sun has gone to bed, and now it is your turn. Sweet dreams.

Good Boy Lukey & the Dream Crumbs

Once upon a time there was a dog named Lukey, and he was the goodest boy.

He had magical powers and would bring all the children joy.

His mommy knew he was special when Lukey was a pup.

If she had bad dreams,
she was always happy
when she woke up.

When Lukey was a
bigger boy, his mommy
had a baby named Grace.

Lukey slept under the
baby's crib every night
in his special place.

Gracie always woke
up happy, with crumbs
in her eyes.

At night when she'd drift
off to sleep is when
Lukey would rise.

You see Lukey's magic power is to keep children out of harm's way.

He protects and keeps them safe so they wake up happy each day.

He gently
sprinkles
dream
crumbs over
sleeping
children's
eyes.

So that any bad
dreams quickly
meet their demise.

He makes
sure that
nightmares
turn happy
and sweet.

with a sprinkle
of dream
crumbs for
every child he
meets

So next time you wake
up with eye crumbles
on your face

Sweet dreams and good snuggles as you drift off at night

Good Boy Lukey
and the dream
crumbs will
make everything
all right.

Made in United States
North Haven, CT
23 July 2023

39433136R00015